Lights Out

ARTHUR GEISERT

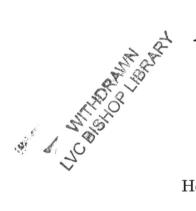

Houghton Mifflin Company Boston 2005

Walter Lorraine Books

For Noah

Walter Lorraine (wr) Books

Copyright © 2005 by Arthur Geisert

www.houghtonmifflinbooks.com

Library of Congress Cataloging-in-Publication Data

Geisert, Arthur.
  Lights out / Arthur Geisert.
      p. cm.
  "Walter Lorraine books."
  Summary: Told by his parents that his light must be out at eight o'clock, a
young piglet who is afraid of the dark devises an ingenious solution to the
problem.
  ISBN-13: 978-0-618-47892-7 (hardcover)
  ISBN-10: 0-618-47892-2 (hardcover)
  [1. Fear of the dark—Fiction. 2. Bedtime—Fiction. 3. Inventions—Fiction.
4. Pigs—Fiction.] I. Title.
  PZ7.G2724Lig 2005
  [E]—dc22
                                                          2005000555

Printed in the United States of America
BVG 10 9 8 7 6 5 4 3 2 1

LIGHTS OUT

My parents make me turn off the light at
eight. They know I'm afraid to go to sleep
unless the light is on. They said, "If you can
figure something out—go ahead." So I did.

4

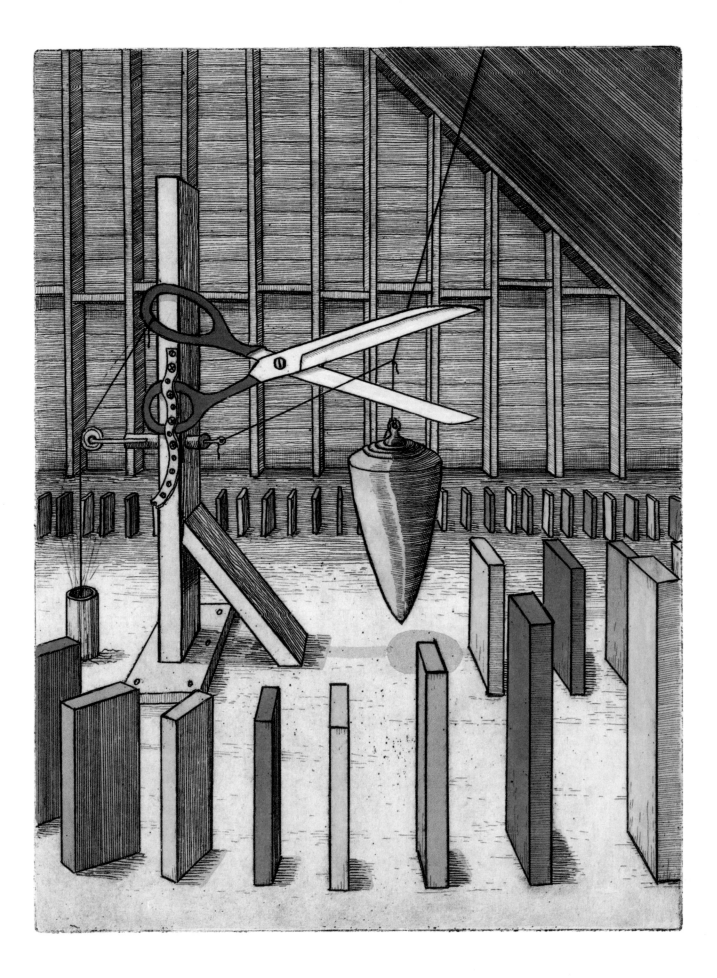

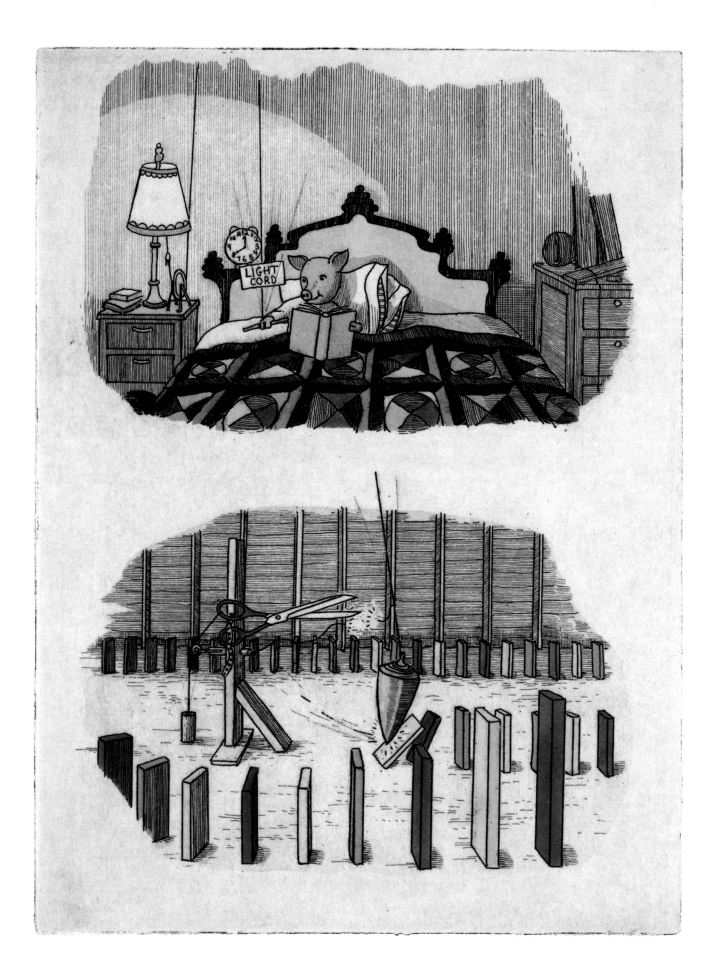

13

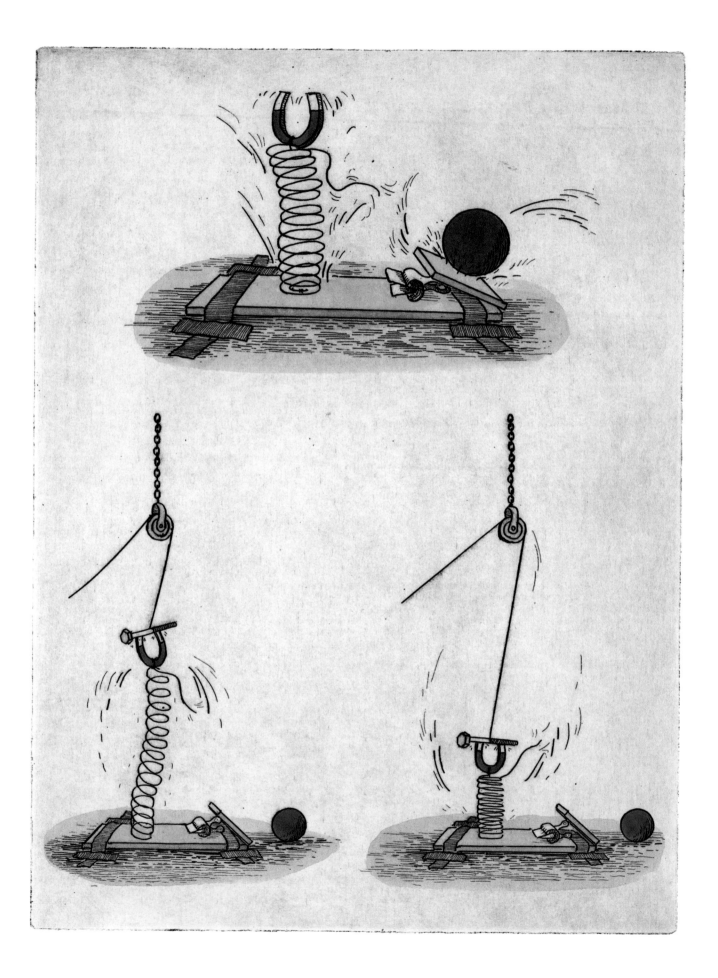

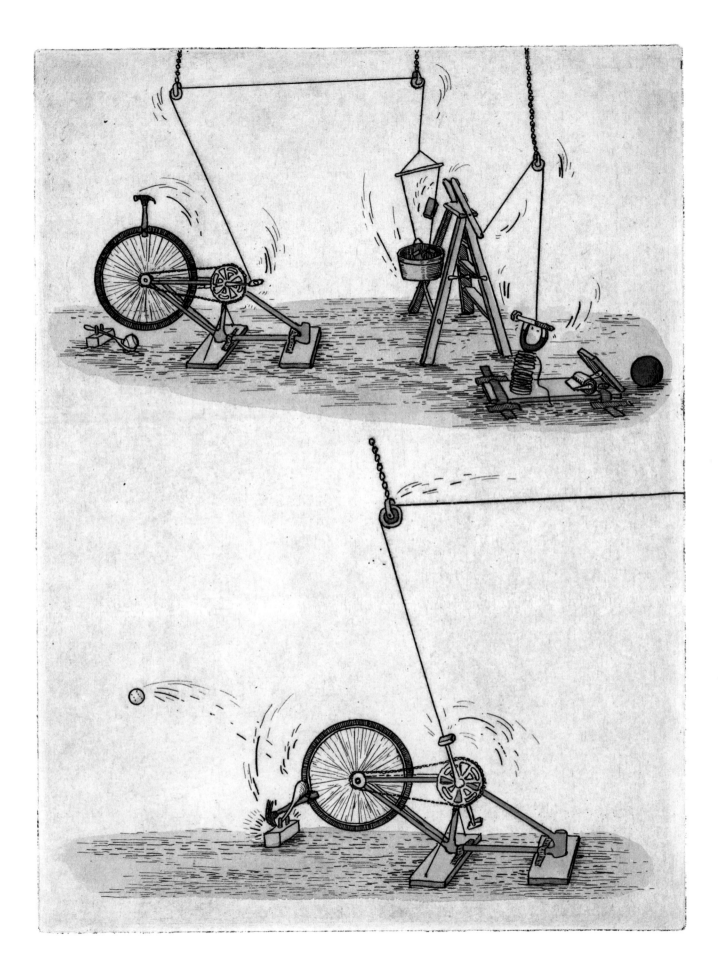

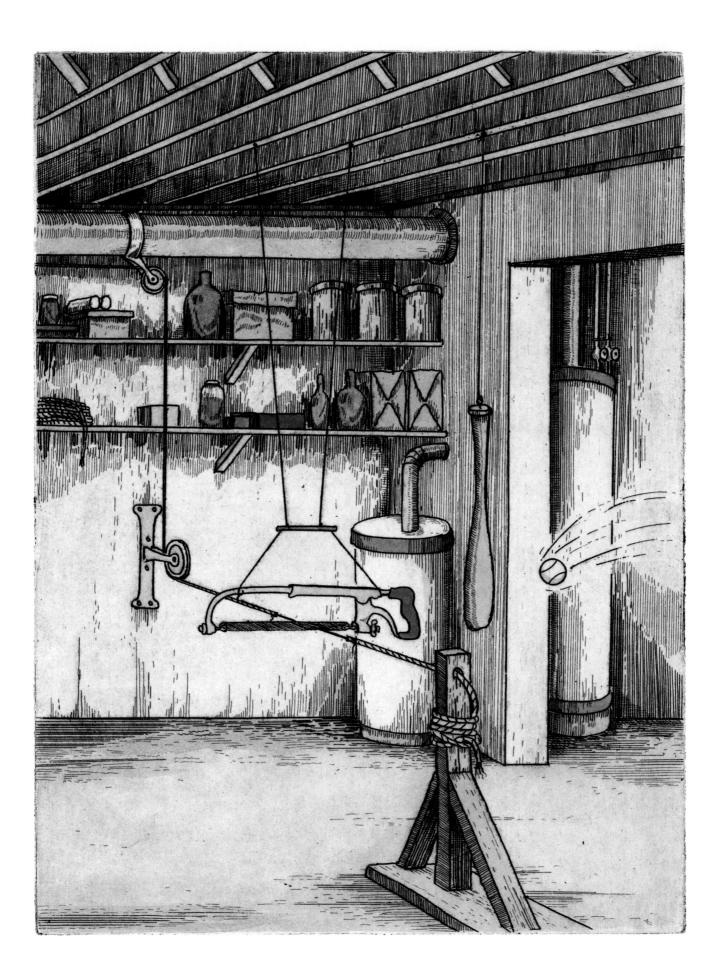

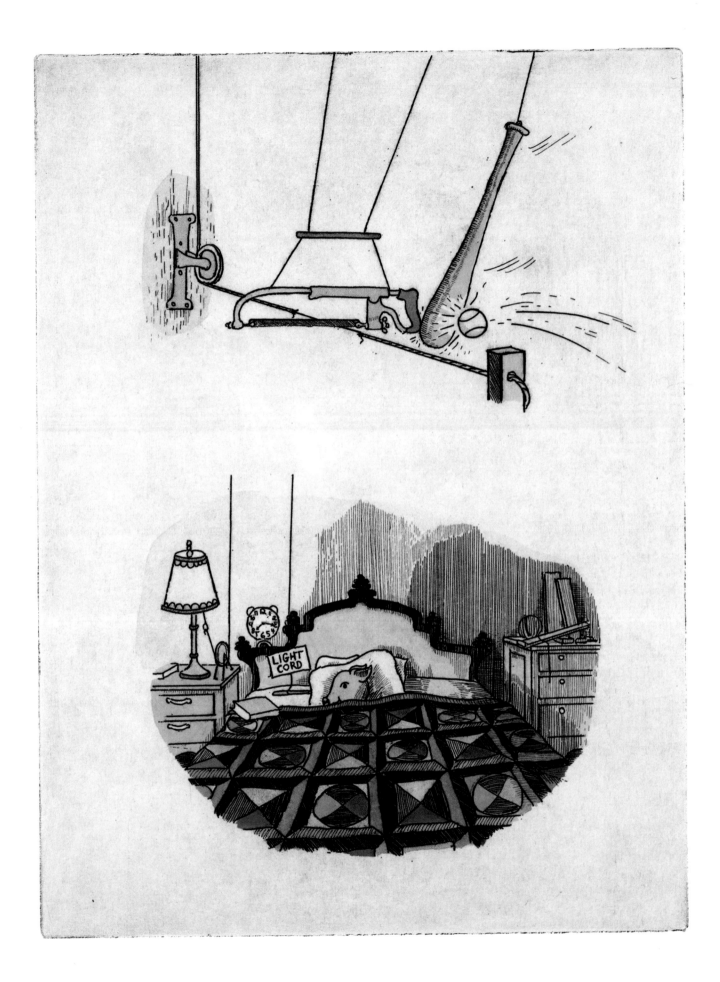

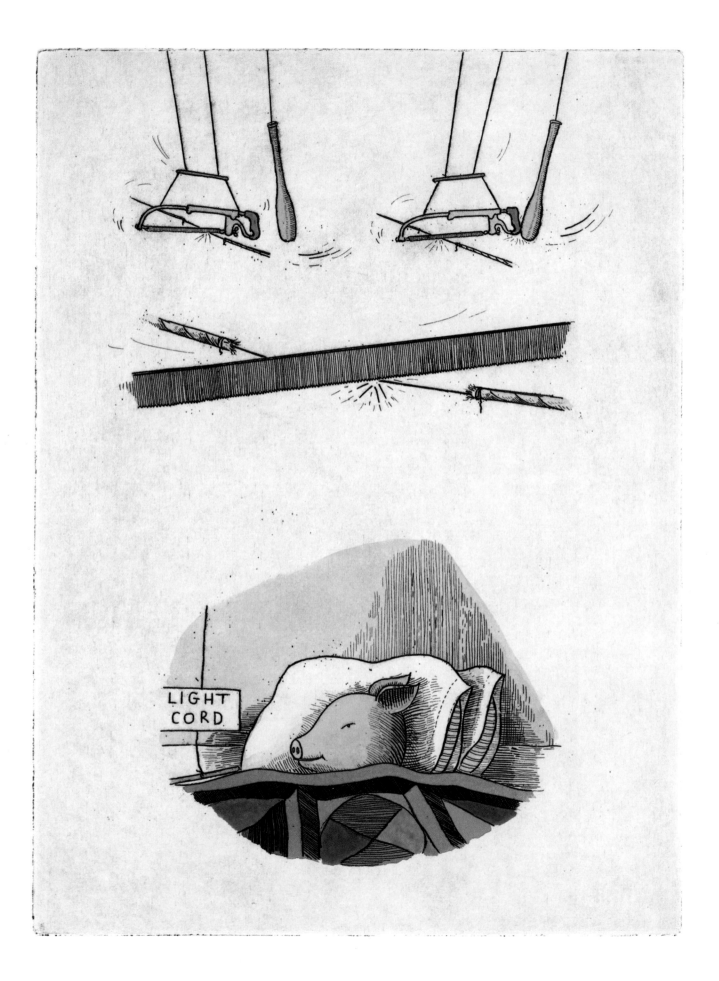

LIGHT
CORD

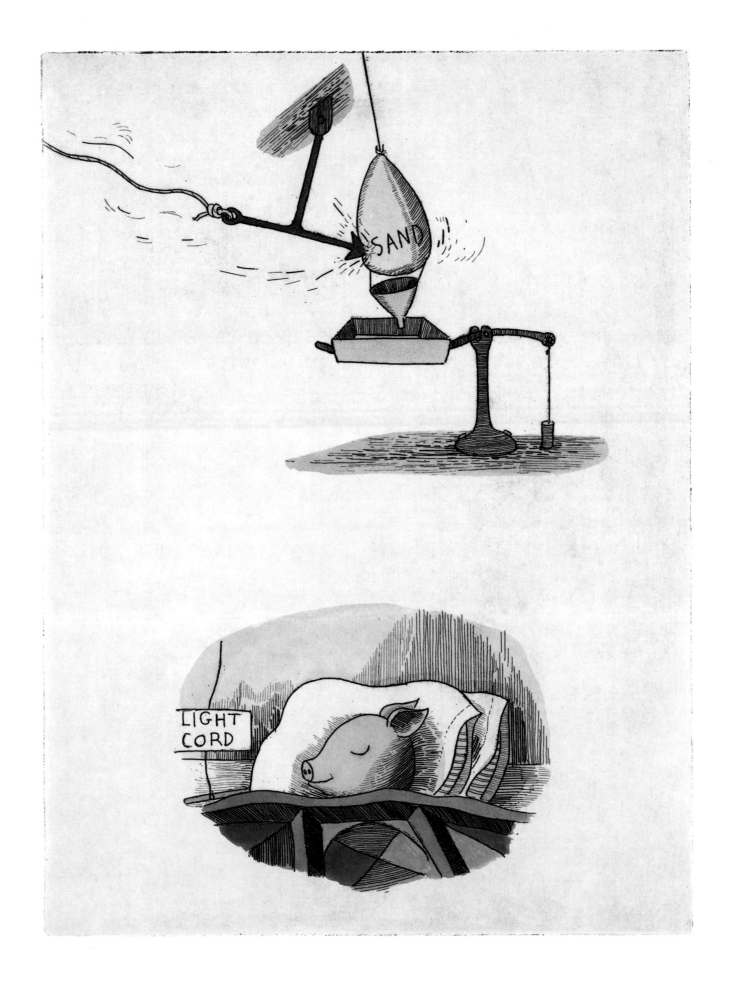

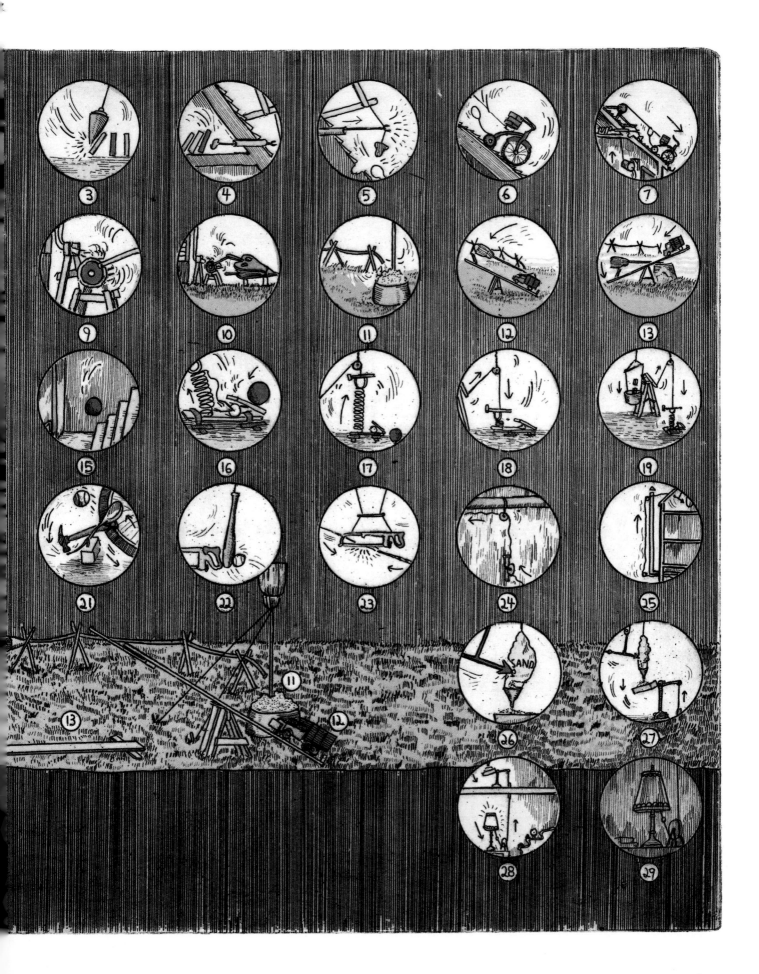

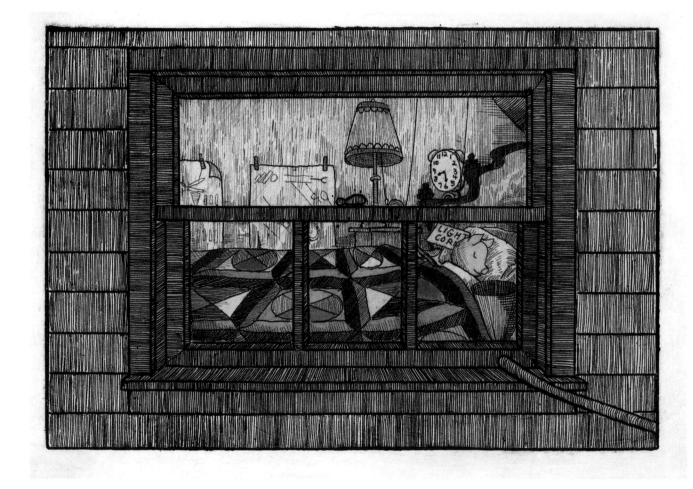

32